AF228480

FORD MUSTANG

Elsie Olson

Big Buddy Books

An Imprint of Abdo Publishing
abdobooks.com

abdobooks.com

Published by Abdo Publishing, a division of ABDO, PO Box 398166, Minneapolis, Minnesota 55439. Copyright © 2021 by Abdo Consulting Group, Inc. International copyrights reserved in all countries. No part of this book may be reproduced in any form without written permission from the publisher. Big Buddy Books™ is a trademark and logo of Abdo Publishing.

Printed in the United States of America, North Mankato, Minnesota
082020
012021

Design: Christa Schneider, Mighty Media, Inc.
Production: Mighty Media, Inc.
Editor: Megan Borgert-Spaniol

Cover Photograph: Shutterstock Images

Interior Photographs: dave_7/Flickr, pp. 10, 11; Doug Coldwell/Wikimedia Commons, p. 28 (1964); GT42CWR-MP/Wikimedia Commons, p. 28 (1994); John Lloyd/Flickr, pp. 8, 9; SenseiAlan/Flickr, pp. 17, 28 (1970s); Shutterstock Images, pp. 4, 5, 18, 19, 20, 21, 22, 23, 24, 25, 26, 27, 29; Sicnag/Flickr, pp. 12, 13, 14, 15; Wikimedia Commons, p. 7

Design Elements: Shutterstock Images

Library of Congress Control Number: 2020931628
Publisher's Cataloging-in-Publication Data
Names: Olson, Elsie, author.
Title: Ford Mustang / by Elsie Olson
Description: Minneapolis, Minnesota : Abdo Publishing, 2021 | Series: Mighty muscle cars | Includes online resources and index
Identifiers: ISBN 9781532193279 (lib. bdg.) | ISBN 9781098211912 (ebook)
Subjects: LCSH: Muscle cars--Juvenile literature. | Motor vehicles--Juvenile literature. | Automobiles--Customizing--Juvenile literature. | Hot rods--Juvenile literature.
Classification: DDC 629.222--dc23

CONTENTS

ZOOM!

A Ford Mustang idles up to the start line. To its left is a Chevy Camaro. Camaros and Mustangs are both known for ruling the drag strip.

Green lights flash. The Mustang's engine roars. It takes off so fast, the front tires rise off the strip! In just eight seconds, the quarter-mile (0.4 km) race is over. The Mustang wins!

DID YOU KNOW?

In a drag race, two cars race on a straight track called a drag strip. Most drag strips are one-eighth mile (0.2 km) or one-quarter mile (0.4 km) long.

FORD MUSTANG

AMERICAN MUSCLE

The Ford Mustang is considered by many to be a top muscle car. Muscle cars are American high-performance cars. They are built for power and speed.

The first muscle car came out in 1949. Muscle cars soon became widely popular in the 1960s. They were made for drag racing. But most could also be driven on city streets.

FORD MUSTANG FAST FACTS

Manufacturer: Ford

First model year: 1964

Top speed: 200 miles per hour (322 km/h)

Top horsepower: 760 hp

Top acceleration: 0 to 60 miles per hour
(96 km/h) in 3.3 seconds

A FORD FIRST

Henry Ford founded Ford Motor Company in 1904. The company quickly became known for its Ford Model T. This affordable model was the most popular car of the early 1900s.

In 1961, Ford's general manager, Lee Iacocca, had an idea. He wanted to make a special kind of car. It would be fast and sporty. But it would also be small, light, and affordable. Iacocca's vision became the first Mustang!

A 1962 model of the Mustang at the Henry Ford Museum in Dearborn, Michigan

THE PONY IS BORN

In 1964, Iacocca's dream became reality. The Mustang was released! The car was like no other on the market. It was sleek. It was stylish. And it was fast!

With the Mustang, Ford had also invented a whole new class of cars. The Mustang is often considered the first pony car. Pony cars are stylish but affordable **coupes**. They have long hoods and short rear decks.

DID YOU KNOW?

The Mustang was named after the World War II P-51 Mustang fighter plane.

The first Mustang was released halfway through 1964. Because of this, many people refer to the first model year as 1964½!

DEBUT YEAR

Ford launched its new car with a bang. The Mustang **debuted** at the 1964 World's Fair in New York City. A Mustang was also the **pace car** at the 1964 Indianapolis 500 race.

The Mustang got even more attention when it appeared in the 1964 James Bond movie *Goldfinger*. The car was a hit with buyers too. Dealers could barely keep the Mustang in stock!

The 1964 Indianapolis 500
Ford Mustang pace car

SHELBY STYLE

The Mustang was a success. But Ford wasn't done yet. In 1965, the company hired driver and car **designer** Carroll Shelby. He made big changes to the Mustang.

Shelby dropped two of the Mustang's four seats. He put in bigger tires and a more powerful engine. The new Mustang wasn't just built to race. It was built to win.

DID YOU KNOW?

Many 1965 Mustang buyers asked not to get its signature paint stripes. This was because police officers were known to target cars with stripes when pulling drivers over for speeding!

Shelby's 1965 Mustang came in white with blue stripes.

CHANGES AND CHALLENGES

People loved the Mustang. But competing carmakers were catching up. Ford had to keep making changes to stay ahead.

Then in the 1970s, the US government made new laws for carmakers. These rules aimed to reduce **pollution**. Because of this, 1970s Mustangs were less powerful than previous models. At the same time, Japanese car models were becoming popular in the US. The Mustang had even more cars to compete with.

1975 Ford Mustang II.
V-8 Optional. Excitement standard.

The success car of '74 is doing it again. In its first year Mustang II outsold all its so-called "competition," combined. And for '75, we've made Mustang II more exciting than ever.

Start with the standards.
• The Mach 1 standard engine is a short stroke 2.8 liter V-6 that delivers surprising performance and fuel economy.

• Staggered rear shocks.
• Front disc brakes.
• Styled steel wheels.
• Dual racing mirrors.
• Full instrumentation.
• Tachometer.
• Contoured bucket seats.
• Passenger and cargo area carpeting.

the work for you or can be shifted manually. This combination puts more options to make your Mach 1 look and handle just the way you want.

More of course. Look close at all the Mustang II models for '75. The Mach 1, the elegant Ghia, the classic 2-door hardtop and the sporty 3-door 2 + 2.

PONY POWER

The Mustang didn't undergo any major **redesigns** through the 1980s. But in 1994, Ford revealed an all-new, restyled Mustang. The car blended its **classic** look with modern elements and improved **technology**.

Ford kept up the pace. From 2005 to 2015, it gave the Mustang two more major redesigns. Each **generation** improved speed, safety, power, and handling. In 2020, Ford **debuted** the Shelby GT500.

The 2005 redesign launched the Mustang's fifth generation. The redesign was meant to attract new, younger buyers as well as people who loved the classic design.

UNDER THE HOOD

FORD MUSTANG SHELBY GT500

The 2020 Ford Mustang Shelby GT500 was the most powerful mass-produced car Ford had ever built. It came with a V8 engine. That means it had eight **cylinders**. Previous Mustang models had four-cylinder engines. The more cylinders an engine has, the more powerful it is.

CAR ENGINES 101

Car engines turn the energy in gasoline into motion. Fuel and air are pumped into the engine's **cylinders**. A spark creates an explosion. The explosion pushes the **piston** down to turn the **crankshaft**. This is a bit like a foot pushing down on a bicycle pedal. At high speed, these explosions happen thousands of times a minute!

ROARING RACES

The Mustang has been an icon on the racetrack since its very first year. In 1964, Mustangs took first and second place in their class at the Tour de France rally race.

Since then, drivers have raced Mustangs on roads, closed tracks, and more. Ford **designs** different Mustang models for specific styles of racing.

DID YOU KNOW?

In rally and road races, drivers compete on paved public or private roads. In stock car races, cars drive laps around a closed racetrack. In drifting races, drivers purposefully lose control of their cars to skid around curves.

A Mustang flies off the ground at a 2011 stock car race in Nevada.

MUSTANG MANIA

Mustangs have become icons on the big screen as well as the racetrack. A Mustang played an important role in the 1974 movie *Gone in 60 Seconds*. It also showed up in a 2000 remake of the film.

Characters in the 2006 movie *Fast and Furious: Tokyo Drift* rebuild a 1967 Mustang. A Mustang even appeared in the hit 2001 Disney film *The Princess Diaries.*

A toy model of the *Fast and Furious* Mustang

ELECTRIC FUTURE

As **technology** improves, the Mustang continues to blaze trails. In late 2019, Ford announced it was coming out with its first electric car. And it would be a Mustang!

The Mustang Mach-E could drive up to 300 miles (483 km) on a full **battery**. Because it was electric, it was much quieter than previous Mustangs. So, Ford included a drive mode that recreates the Mustang's **signature** engine growl. Ford's iconic car is racing toward the future!

The Mach-E was the first four-door Mustang. It was also the first Mustang to offer all-wheel drive.

Henry Ford founded the Ford Motor Company.

1904

Because of US **pollution** laws, Mustangs made in the 1970s were less powerful than previous models.

1970s

1964

The Ford Mustang **debuted** at the World's Fair.

1994

Ford revealed an all-new, restyled Mustang.

Ford presented its sixth-generation Mustang.

2015

Ford **debuted** the Mustang Shelby GT500, the most powerful Mustang yet.

2020

2005

Another major **redesign** launched the fifth Mustang **generation**.

2019

Ford announced plans for the Mustang Mach-E, the company's first electric car.

GLOSSARY

battery—a small container filled with chemicals that makes electrical power.

classic—something that has been considered excellent for a long time.

coupe—a car with a fixed roof, two doors, and two or four seats.

crankshaft—a long, metal rod that transfers energy from the engine through the transmission and eventually to the wheels.

cylinder—a shaft in which a piston of an engine moves.

debut—to appear for the first time or present something for the first time.

design (dih-ZINE)—to plan how something will appear or work. A redesign is a change in the way an existing thing appears or works. A designer is someone who plans how something will appear or work.

generation—a class of objects created from an earlier type.

pace car—a car that leads competing race cars during warm-up laps. A pace car also enters the track during a race to slow the pace if there are hazardous conditions.

piston—a part in an engine that moves up and down inside the cylinder.

pollution—human waste that dirties or harms air, water, or land.

signature—something that sets apart or identifies an individual, group, or company.

technology (tehk-NAH-luh-jee)—a capability given by the practical application of knowledge.

World War II—a war fought in Europe, Asia, and Africa from 1939 to 1945.

ONLINE RESOURCES

To learn more about the Ford Mustang, please visit **abdobooklinks.com** or scan this QR code. These links are routinely monitored and updated to provide the most current information available.

INDEX